EATS

DATE DUE

EATS

Poems by Arnold Adoff
illustrated by Susan Russo

Mulberry Books, New York

Copyright © 1979 by Arnold Adoff. All rights reserved. No part of this book may be
reproduced or utilized in any form or by any means, electronic or mechanical, includ-
ing photocopying, recording or by any information storage and retrieval system, with-
out permission in writing from the Publisher. Inquiries should be addressed to
Lothrop, Lee & Shepard Books, a division of William Morrow & Company, Inc., 1350
Avenue of the Americas, New York, NY 10019. Printed in the United States of
America. First Mulberry Edition, 1992.   1 2 3 4 5 6 7 8 9 10
Library of Congress Cataloging in Publication Data.   Adoff, Arnold.   Eats.
SUMMARY: Reflections on the poet's love of food and eating.   1. Food–Juvenile poet-
ry.   [1. Food–Poetry.   2. American Poetry]   I. Russo, Susan.   II. Title.
PZ8.3.A233Eat   811'.5'4   79-11300   ISBN 0-688-11695-7

Recipe For Eats Poems

Take One Grandma Ida in a warm kitchen smelling
        of Russian Coffee Cake and Gorky
add   One Mother Rita in a warm kitchen smelling
        of French Toast and Maupassant
combine
with One Wife Virginia
                        in a warm kitchen smelling
        of Plum Sauce and Gertrude Stein
season
with Two Children Jaime and Leigh
                        in a warm kitchen smelling
        of Brown Bread and Milne
place
inside A Poet$_s$ head and cook for a long time
then
serve with the enthusiasm of An Editor Dorothy
            to hungry Readers ready for the taste

Eats

    are on my mind   from early morning
      to late at night
                 in spring
                 or winter
    there is
      no wrong
      or right
        time
      to feel that sudden
              need
      to find that sudden
              meal

i am always hungry

Not Me But

cows walk up and beg to
be
burgers
chicken legs
will tap dance
to
my
teeth
and
oatmeal cookies
have
been
known
to fly
out of their jars
as i pass by

My Mouth

stays shut
            but
food   just
finds
        a way

                my tongue says
we are
        full today
        but
            teeth just
                    grin
        and
        say
            come in

i am always hungry

Love
Song

great goblets of pudding powder in milk
hot with marshmallows on a winter afternoon
syrup on vanilla ice cream frosting on cake
a kind of cake dripping to dry on warm
doughnuts fresh from the oven candy
                                    candy bars
bars chunks thick and broken pieces squares
spoons and pots and lots
                    before brushing
fudge and milk
      and german and sour cream
light and dark and bitter sweet and
                              even
                              white

      you are no good
                    for me
      you are no good

      you are so good

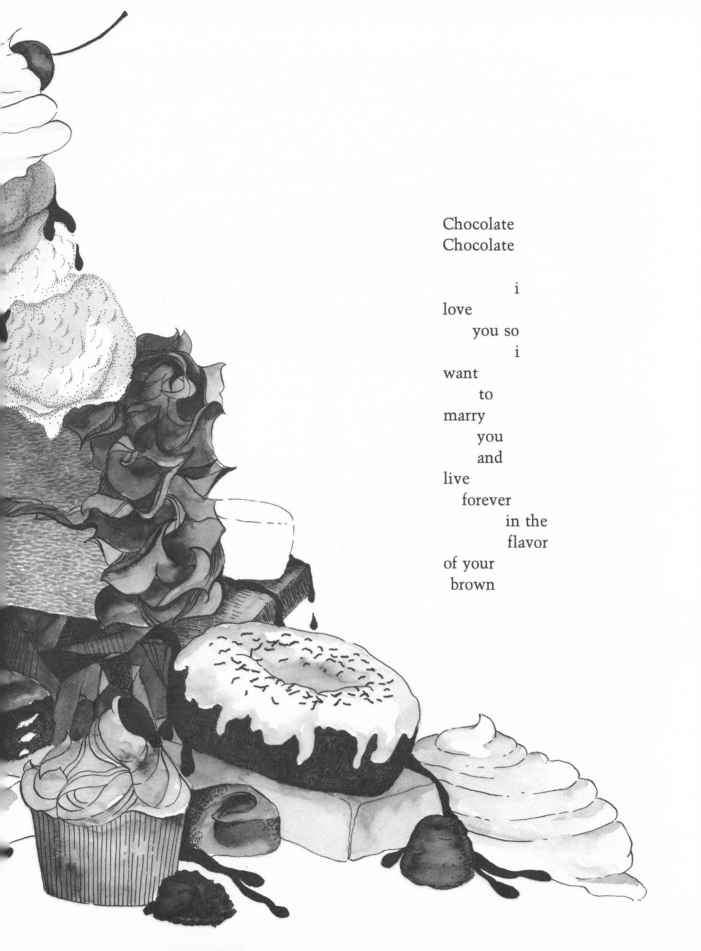

Chocolate
Chocolate

        i
love
   you so
       i
want
    to
marry
    you
    and
live
  forever
      in the
       flavor
of your
  brown

Measuring and Mixing

i am
beating
breakfast
by
myself

only
assisted
         by
one
sleepy
and
older
     sister

     waiting
          for
          an
     accident

After All The Digging

                         and the planting
                         and the   pulling
of weeds
          on hot summer afternoons

there are cool mornings
we can
          walk between
the rows
          and bite a bean   or chew a lettuce
                                        leaf
          and taste the ripe tomatoes
the
way
the rabbits
              take
    breakfast

Getting The Sweet

                         strawberries
from my
fingers
      down
      into the basket
without
        eating all of them
                   up
                  is
      the problem

      the solution
            is
            not
       to solve
      the problem
until
     you
       are
     full
      of answers

The Apple

         is on the top
branch
    of the tree
        touching
the
sky
    or the apple is
        in
    the
    sky
touching
    the top branch
      of the tree

and i am
    me on the ground
    waiting
       for
        a
   good
   wind

Take One Apple

                                   wash and
                                            dry

and
eat
    it   up and down
                    and side
                          ways

to
the
core

                then
                take

                    one
                    apple
                    more

Take One

old apple tree   and climb and shake
and pick enough apples   to fill one
large
grocery bag
then carry them
inside
and begin to work

cut out the core   of seeds
cut the apples in half
cut out the worms and bugs
peel and slice
thin

then follow your best family recipe for pie
or cobbler or tarts or cake or crisp   or pie
or crunch or turnovers or dumplings or pie

get help on everything but the eating

At The End Of Summer

                  when the old tree   is full
                  and leaning to the ground
                  with its heavy load
i pledge my loyalty
              to apple pie
                    and

i insist on deep
        done dough
as heavy as gold
as golden
        as sweet sun
             and
                no other
      of this
           natural   world

unless
      there is a peach or rhubarb national
      emergency   or mince and pumpkin flooding
      in the fall   and the president calls
      to ask
          will you please do your share
              and eat for dear america

      wild berry in the spring   chocolate
        cream   or boston dream and
                      all
      the other flavors that
                  wake
      me shaking in the night
                  are
      only tasty second best

until
      each end of summer
                  when i pledge
      my loyalty again to
            apple
only
      and always
            apple

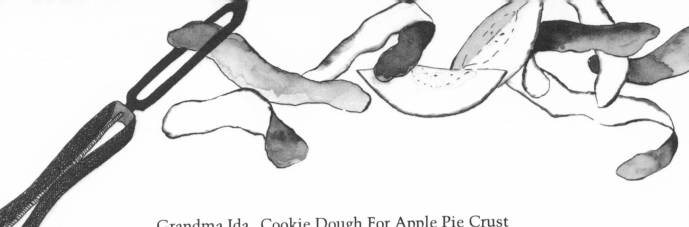

Grandma Ida$_s$ Cookie Dough For Apple Pie Crust

mix in a large bowl   ½ cup sugar
                        ½ cup oil
                        2 eggs   until they are creamed

add   2 tablespoons orange juice
        ½ teaspoon vanilla   and stir well

sift together   2½ cups flour
                  2 teaspoons baking powder
                                    and
add this flour combination to the
creamy liquid   but do it slow   then stir until you have
                                    a soft ball of dough

cover with a kitchen towel and place in refrigerator
        from 2 to 12 hours   until you are ready for pie
then grease and flour a pan   spread out half of the dough
        ball until you have a bottom crust for your pie

or you can flour a board and roll out the dough to make
        two crusts   a bottom is a bottom   but a top can
        be strips of dough   or one whole crust

just   get your apples and begin

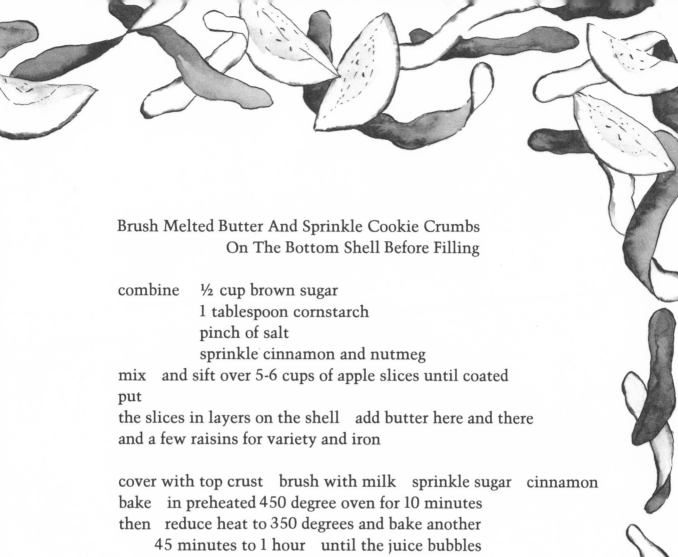

Brush Melted Butter And Sprinkle Cookie Crumbs
         On The Bottom Shell Before Filling

combine   ½ cup brown sugar
              1 tablespoon cornstarch
              pinch of salt
              sprinkle cinnamon and nutmeg
mix   and sift over 5-6 cups of apple slices until coated
put
the slices in layers on the shell   add butter here and there
and a few raisins for variety and iron

cover with top crust   brush with milk   sprinkle sugar   cinnamon
bake   in preheated 450 degree oven for 10 minutes
then   reduce heat to 350 degrees and bake another
     45 minutes to 1 hour   until the juice bubbles
     through the holes in the top crust
                                   and the smell
o the smell

Thank You

              after the buds and the blossoms
              and the apples grown full of juice
         you
         can   on an august morning   after your
                                   belly is full

         give the old tree a hug

Hard

is
in
  the
middle
  of
  a
carrot
  on
  a
loose

tooth

Soft

is
on
  a
  bed
with
book
a
pillow
for my
head
  and
quiet

Raisins
  in
  one
hand

Dinner Tonight

                    is hiding
in a mystery of steam
from
        the bowl of
spaghetti
                    and meat sauce
                    and
we
        must make our way through
        oregano fogs
                        and the deadly smog
                        of a grated   cheese
                                          breeze
        into a parmesan dream

past
        snapping beans and over broccoli logs
        we are in pizza country
                and there is danger
                                    of
                                    pepperoni
                                    poisoning
        until dessert

The Baker

        wanted me to know
that
    underneath   the cheese
             and
    sausage bits
         and
    pepperoni
      slices   and beneath the onions
         and mushrooms and green
                pepper
                 dices
the only thing that counted
was
the
   dough

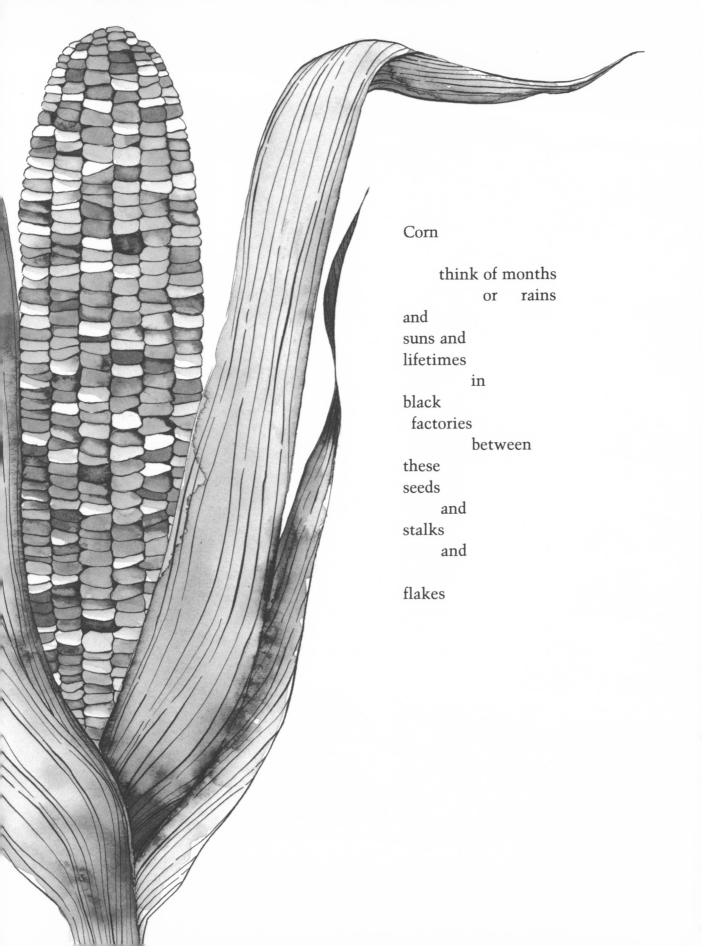

Corn

       think of months
             or   rains
and
suns and
lifetimes
        in
black
  factories
           between
these
seeds
      and
stalks
      and

flakes

Burger

        back
         up
seven
spaces
        into
         my
mouth
        do
        not
pass

        go

After Covering

        the continent
of north america
in
   sugar   and bombing all
              our
   cities
      into surrender
            with their yellow cakes

the giant   landed on the white house lawn
     Twinkie
          and
           cream
         filled
          creatures
demanded all our
      broccoli as their price
              for
         peace

Sun Flowers

            they are so beautiful
in perfect
            circle
            rows
inside
      their collars of green
                  leaves

      we hate to pick
            their seeds
                  out
                  for
            the oven pan

      they will roast
            slowly
and
dry   to the
            taste
      of autumn
sun

Cut
Out

an ugly face   with triangle eyes
and a big   tooth   mouth   for the
                              candle   glow
then scrape the seeds
                          out
                          and
wash them
          and put them
in a flat and shallow
                    pan
in a low oven
              for as long as you can wait
                        this dark night

when they are done baking
                          you
                            eat
                be fore
                booing

Under

this autumn sky   i think of these
ingredients when they were rooted
in the ground
                    that pound of flour
                                        as
                some stalks
                            of wheat
        this sugar as
                        sweet
            sugar canes or beets

            even the chicken eggs
            and salt and rising
                                yeast

i always use this wooden spoon to stir
                        the batter for the bread
it was
            once a tree   or part of a tree
                        rooted in the ground
under
        the
        sky

Turn The Oven On
                    To 350 Degrees   and Grease
                    A Deep And Round Baking Pan

first   combine in a large bowl   2 cups unsifted flour
                                      2 envelopes dry yeast
                                      1 tablespoon salt
                                      ¼ cup sugar

then   heat in a small pot
                         1 cup milk
                         1 cup water
                         ¼ cup oil
until you have a warm liquid
            that is not too hot

            mix this warm liquid   and 2 eggs
                    into the flour combination
blend
until the yeast is dissolved

use a wooden spoon to stir into the bowl
            another 2½ cups of flour
then keep stirring until you have a bowl
                        of stiff batter

Cover The Bowl With A Kitchen Towel

put in a warm place   and let the dough rise
for an hour   then stick your wooden spoon
into the dough and stir it down   and spoon
                              it into your pan

bake for 45 minutes   until the loaf begins to brown
then
take it out of the oven and brush on an Egg Wash or
                                             Dorure

              of   1 egg yolk
                              beaten with
                    2 tablespoons of milk
                       and a pinch of salt
then
bake again until golden brown

              remove from oven

                       cool
                       down

Good For The Head

              when you need more
                  sleep
but
you are sitting at the breakfast
      table
         instead
not
   ready for school

            some quiet
              cream
            of
            peanut
             butter
on a piece
         of
natural
      brown
      bread

Peanut Butter Batter Bread

mix in a large bowl   1 cup unsifted flour
                             ½ cup instant oats
                             ½ cup yellow cornmeal
                             ½ cup sugar
                             ½ cup powdered milk
                             3 teaspoons baking powder
                             1 teaspoon salt

when they are all stirred together well
     add 2/3 cup peanut butter (either kind)
     and combine until the pieces are small
then
beat 2 eggs and 1½ cups milk (liquid)
     add to flour mixture   stir well
pour
into greased and floured 9x5x3 bread pan

bake in preheated 325 degree oven for an hour

remove   cool   spread   eat

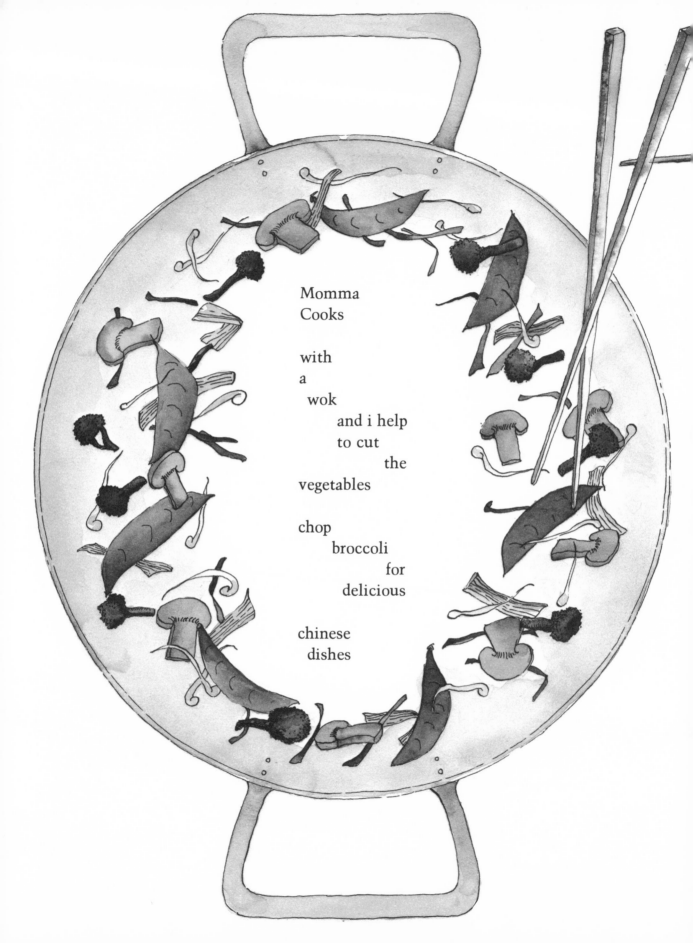

Momma
Cooks

with
a
  wok
     and i help
    to cut
       the
vegetables

chop
  broccoli
     for
   delicious

chinese
  dishes

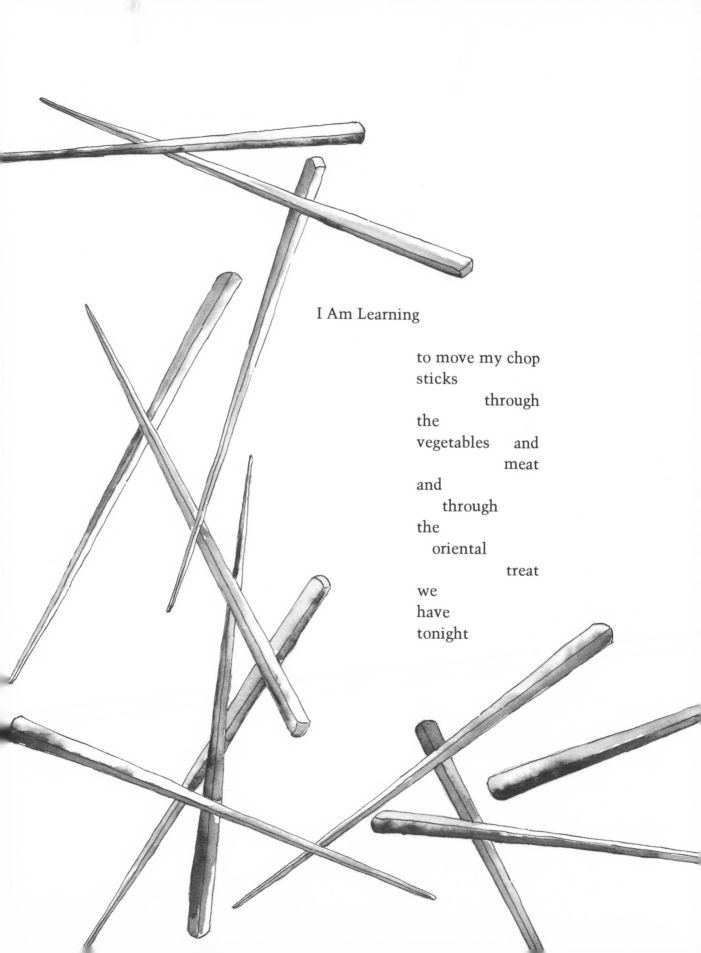

I Am Learning

to move my chop
sticks
                through
the
vegetables   and
                    meat
and
        through
the
    oriental
                    treat
we
have
tonight

but   in
between
        my
        smiles
        and
        bites

i
write
a
message
            in
            the
sweet
        and
sour
pork

i
need
a
    fork

Deep Into Winter

                         before the January thaw
when the snow
               is a foot high   in our field
               and crusted   with thick ice
and
the berries are gone from the buckthorn
                              and wild rose

the rabbits begin to eat the bark of young   trees
     the yellow apple   the korean cherry bushes
                         and even the redbud saplings
leaving long tooth circles around their trunks

stopping to chew and listen
                              their famous ears
                              are straight up
their noses   point to the safety of the hedge

their eyes in our direction

Just

       when winter spreads out
       across the fields   and it is colder
than   we remember cold

here
come   tangerines   rolling up from Florida
onto   the market shelves

                   an orange army

almost
       by themselves
they
       are
       the
         seeds of spring

There Is A Place

on
the couch
        for
        grandma
and
a place on
        grandma
for
  me

  in front
of
the
  fire
     and pop
        ping
        corn

The Coach Said

                      i had
                        the
youngest
roundest
            belly
he
had ever felt

was
    un
nec
    ess
    ary

          for basketball

The New Pants

              i found
under the
        christmas
           tree
two
  weeks
ago

are hardly worn
but
     split on me
          yesterday
as
i caught the long bomb
and was trying
       to
        go
all
the
way

I Love To Eat   I Love To Eat
     What

and
i love to eat   a lot
    of all
    of that
      but
i am
    growing tall
        not
         fat
and my
   eyes are almost to the shelf
   my hands can reach
          for
         the
  extra treats each
        after
      noon

soon
   i will be grown